FOUL PLAY

JOHN KELLY

Books by John Kelly

First published 2021 by Macmillan Children's Books
an imprint of Pan Macmillan
The Smithson, 6 Briset Street, London EC1M 5NR
EU representative: Macmillan Publishers Ireland Ltd,
1st Floor, The Liffey Trust Centre,
117–126 Sheriff Street Upper, Dublin 1 D01 YC43
Associated companies throughout the world
www.panmacmillan.com

ISBN 978-1-5290-2129-5

135798642

A CIP catalogue record for this book is available
from the British Library.

Printed and bound by CPI Group (UK) Ltd, Croydon CR0 4YY

MIX
Paper from
responsible sources
FSC® C016486
FSC
www.fsc.org

To all the monster players
on the other team.

CONTENTS:

A GHASTLY COLOUR COMBINATION

Chapter 1

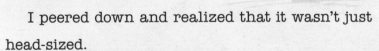

I had just turned the corner into Lovecraft Avenue when a head-sized object came *flying* through the air towards me. Without thinking, I caught it.

I peered down and realized that it wasn't just head-sized.

It actually was a head.

A **scruffy, *smelly* and smiley head** with a friendly face I recognized at once.

'Hello, Morty!' I said. 'Where's the rest of you today?' My friend Morty is a Level-1 registered dead person (a zombie to you) and therefore his arms, legs, eyeballs and belly-buttons were regularly falling off.

'Oh! Hello Ozzy!' Morty replied, grinning up at me with his **gap-toothed mouth**. 'Never mind that now – what a lovely catch! **Bravo!** I didn't know you were playing.'

'Playing what?' I asked confusedly.

Morty plays a lot of sports. In fact, one of the reasons his body parts are often in several places at once is because he's always felt that being dead shouldn't get in the way of his hobbies.

He plays **MUGBALL** (monster rugby), **zombie football, mixed monster martial arts** (MMMA) and – on one memorable but catastrophic occasion – he even went **bungee-jumping.**

'Why, we're playing, **MONSTERBALL**, of course!' Morty laughed. 'Surely you know that today is the **Dimension 3 MONSTERBALL CHAMPIONSHIP FINAL?'**

I looked at him blankly, as I always do whenever anyone mentions human sports like Stick-Whack, Baskethoop or Runny-jump thing. I forget their names.

You see, I'm about as fond of human sports as I am of scraping the cheese out from between a troll's toes. So monster sports couldn't be any better.

'Never mind,' continued Morty. 'A few of us thought we'd celebrate Cup Final day by having a nice, friendly amateur game of **MONSTERBALL** here in Lovecraft Avenue.'

'Who is "we"?' I asked. But the words were barely out of my mouth before there was a loud **ROAR** from behind me.

It's rarely a good sign to hear *a loud* ROAR behind you, so I was feeling a tiny bit nervous when I turned round. **A mob of hideously ugly monsters** was charging out of the alleyway that runs down the side of DIG-IT!, the new ghoul fashion boutique.

You might be thinking that I'd be frightened. But after spending the summer working for the monster doctor, the sight of **slobbering jaws, razor-sharp horns** and **quivering eye-stalks** isn't any more frightening to me than my Granny Freda's *sherry-and-lavender-flavoured moustache*. (And being **'hideously ugly'** is completely normal for monsters.)

The mob all sported scarves with the same ghastly colour combination: *Rabid Red and Yahoo Yellow stripes.* I recognized regular patients like **Bob the Blob,** who was slithering rapidly along in a thick slick of his own **snot,** and Mr Gillman,

a swamp creature who'd recently moved into one of the new super-damp basement flats beneath the **snake-grooming parlour.** At the head of the mob was the **fifteen stone of thrashing tentacles, temper and tasteless knitwear**

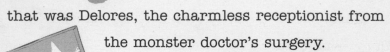

that was Delores, the charmless receptionist from the monster doctor's surgery.

Delores once scored 12.3 on the **inter-dimensional standardized monster grumpiness test** – which is pretty amazing since the test only goes up to 10. So I didn't feel great when she pointed a **quivering tentacle** in my direction and bellowed – in a voice like a T. rex auditioning for the role of an evil pirate captain in a pantomime – 'AWFUL **ALL-STARS! ATTACK!**'

The mob of monsters following her roared in response and charged straight at me.

'Morty,' I said, as calmly as I could manage in the circumstances, 'why are Delores and those patients charging at me?'

Morty grinned. 'They're not charging at YOU, Ozzy.' And before I could check whether his eyes had fallen out again he added, **'They're charging at ME!'**

'Ah!' I said. As if that made the slightest difference. I was, after all, currently holding him. 'Is there any particular reason why?'

I was hoping that he'd come up with some answer that didn't include us both ending up as **flat as Lucy Liverwort** after the *triple-chocolate-toffee-cake* **stampede** in the school canteen last year. Tragic.

'Like I said,' my zombie friend replied, 'we decided to play **MONSTERBALL.** But as the ball said she was feeling a bit sick – someone she ate, apparently – I volunteered to take her place!'

As answers go, that clearly wasn't a great deal of help.

Luckily, the monster doctor had taught me to always keep an eye out for a *potential escape route*, no matter where I was. (This is a vital skill for any trainee monster

doctor. You never know when you'll need a quick getaway from an **angry** or **dissatisfied** patient.) So as the **fangs, horns,** claws and *slobber* of the **AWFUL ALL-STARS** bore down on me, I tucked Morty under my arm and began edging towards an alleyway to my right.

Unfortunately, just as I was about to make a break for it, a second (and just as hideously ugly) mob of monsters erupted from that alleyway too.

Oh, super.

This mob was headed by Vlad, the vampire who runs the all-night convenience store on the corner of Lovecraft Avenue. Tearing after him were his regulars, like Colin the ghoul, Simon Salamander from the **Battered Squid chippy** and Mrs Stunck, a very nice jellified thing who lives in one of the larger bins round the back of the restaurant.

With the depressing inevitability of a bad mark in a maths test, the second mob spotted Morty and howled, **'FANGTOWN FANGTOMS NEVER DIE!'**

Then they put their heads down (or whatever passed for a head) and charged straight for us.

Two monster mobs. Me in the middle.

I groaned in frustration.

It wasn't even the **imminent danger** that was worrying me. After all, a typical day as an assistant monster doctor isn't complete without extreme danger. So far this month I'd been **eaten** and **blown-up,** and I spent most days covered in **foul-smelling bodily fluids.** Last Wednesday I'd even been carried aloft to an impressive height of 17,000ft in the claws of a short-sighted dragon mother who mistook me for her baby draggling!

No. I was frustrated because I hadn't even had a chance to sit down and prepare myself for the day with a nice cup of *coughee* and a chocolate indigestive.

It was so unfair.

I was just wondering if the monster doctor's skills included **reviving a completely flattened human boy,** when I was suddenly distracted by a rubbish bin shouting at me.

SKINBIN

Chapter 2

This probably wasn't the best moment to let myself be distracted by a bin. After all, I had the terrifying forces of Delores's **AWFUL ALL-STARS** charging at me from the left, while from my right thundered Vlad the vampire's **FANGTOWN FANGTOMS.** The very pavement beneath my feet was **shaking with my impending doom.**

But, in my defence, **monster skinbins** are supposed to be impossible to ignore. That's why they are striped with a nasty neon yellow and black pattern that would make a wasp look discreetly dressed. This is so that any monster *about to moult or flick its waste skin all over the pavement* cannot claim they hadn't seen a nearby skinbin.

MiN-MON SKINBIN

Skin littering is a revolting personal habit, a public health hazard and is punishable by fines of up to 200 Karloffz.

Please use the skinbin provided. (For pieces of waste skin larger than one square metre, thicker than 40mm, or armour-plated skin, please visit your local council skin dump.)

**REMEMBER TO KEEP OUR STREETS CLEAN!
IF YOU PICK IT OFF – PICK IT UP!**

TAKE YOUR OWN SKIN HOME!
For more information visit www.pickitoff-pickitup.com

In this instance, the bin was even harder to ignore as it was not alone. There were two of them. One wore a scarf and hat in the **AWFUL ALL-STARS** strip colours, the other wore the colours of the **FANGTOWN FANGTOMS.**

Oh great! Charging mobs of monsters closing in from either side, and now sports-mad skinbins ahead of me.

14

They were both hopping up and down excitedly in front of the monster doctor's surgery, **like toddlers seconds away from a toilet disaster,** waving their tiny little arms at me.

The **AWFUL ALL-STARS** bin shouted, 'OVER HERE! OZZY! PASS IT TO ME!'

'IGNORE HIM! PASS IT TO ME!' yelled the **FANGTOMS** bin, neatly tripping its rival over.

The **AWFUL ALL-STARS** waste disposal monster crashed to the ground, but immediately executed a neat forward roll and acrobatically sprang back to its tiny feet. It then reverse head-butted the charging **FANGTOWN FANGTOM,** which promptly collapsed to the pavement.

'Stay down, Binny!' it said menacingly. 'You're beat.' But the fallen **FANGTOWN FANGTOM** had other ideas. It swept the ALL-STAR legs from underneath it and the two skinbins crashed to the ground on top of each other.

'GET OFF ME, YOU RUBBISH RECEPTACLE!' howled the **FANGTOM.**

'IT WAS ALWAYS MY BALL, YOU CHEATING CONTAINER!' screeched the **ALL-STAR.** They writhed and clashed and clanged for position.

'PASS IT TO ME, OZZY!' shouted the **ALL-STAR.**

'NO! PASS IT TO ME!' squawked the **FANGTOM.**

This was ridiculous. I needed to get Morty's head as far away from me as possible.

I took a quick look at the two mobs of monsters charging down the street towards me, wound my arm back and threw Morty as hard and as far away as I could. But sadly my throw was about as accurate as one of Grandad's **'when-I-was-your-age-young-man'** stories.

I had been aiming for the messy bit of hedge outside **The Earthy Eatery,** the worm-noodle takeaway. But my throw went *completely wide.*

The two battling skinbins were clearly disgusted. 'What a useless throw!' the **FANGTOM** cried.

'Typical human!' agreed the **ALL-STAR,** glaring at me. Then they jumped up and raced off in pursuit of Morty. And, to my relief, so did the two teams of **rampaging monsters.**

But my relief only lasted a moment.

I quickly realized that my throw was arcing across Lovecraft Avenue and heading straight towards Mrs Letterman, the postbox. *It was going to smack her in the back of her head!* **'MRS LETTERMAN!'** I yelled. **'LOOK OUT!'**

The old postbox turned and looked up with surprise at the zombie head flying towards her. She just had time to blurt out, 'What the—?' before years of instinct took over. She opened her letter slot wide, *gulping down Morty's head as if he were a first-class parcel.* (I've since checked with **Monster Mail** and they told me that sending a zombie head by post is fine, as long as it is correctly addressed and has sufficient postage. The human Royal Mail never answered my email.)

I could just make out the muffled sound of Morty's voice shouting,

'OH! LOVELY CATCH, MRS LETTERMAN!'

from inside the post-monster.

Mrs Letterman shouted, *'WAIT!'* and tried to back away from the onrushing mobs of teeth, tusks and tentacles. *'STOP! STOP!'* she shouted.

'STOP! I'M NOT PLAYING YOUR STUPID GA—'

before she was cut off as several tonnes of overly competitive monsters landed on top of her.

I once saw an old black-and-white film of **two steam trains crashing headlong into each other.** This was just like that, but with the **thundering** explosion of steam, steel and railway sleepers replaced by *slime,* **horns** and

the occasional **suddenly detached limb.**

The wreckage of broken monsters that remained was like the aftermath to the world's worst game of **Monster Twister.** Cries of pain and discomfort filled the air.

'AARGGH!' moaned Colin the ghoul. 'I've lost my leg!'

'No you haven't!' groaned Mrs Stunck. 'It's over here.' She pointed at Bob the Blob's head.

Delores snapped, **'If the tentacle poking my left earhole is still there in two seconds its owner is going to lose it!'**

But the howls of pain were cut off suddenly as the door to the surgery banged open.

The monster doctor, Annie von Sichertall MD, stood there in the doorway. She looked **absolutely furious.**

VERY, VERY, VERY MESSY

Chapter 3

'What in the name of **Gorgonzilla's gorgeously gargantuan undergarments** is going on?' cried the monster doctor, her angry voice **booming** out at the tangle of monsters before her. 'What have I told you about playing that *stupid* game around here?'

She stood there, fists planted on her hips, looking *as intimidating as a grizzly bear bouncer at a dodgy grizzly bear nightclub.*

I hadn't seen her this angry for a while.
Not since that time she caught me taking notes
with a sharpened pencil at **BITE NITE,** the
Wednesday evening vampire dental clinic.

She leapt straight into action and began using
her huge ape-like arms to yank the mangled
FANGTOMS and **ALL-STARS** supporters apart.

'OZZY!' she barked. 'Stop standing there
gawping gormlessly. Come over here and give
me a hand with Mrs Effluvium's head. It's wedged
rather firmly somewhere it wasn't designed to go.'

We carried the lump of patients back into the
surgery, and for the next ten minutes
I received a crash course in
untangling monsters.

Which is a bit like separating a plate of cooked spaghetti Bolognese back into three separate piles: one of pasta, one of meat and one of tomatoes. (I'm not saying it can't be done – just that it is **very, very, very messy.)**

Luckily, most monsters are extremely **robust,** which is why twenty minutes later the doctor and I had sent most of the lightly wounded home. I had just finished **gaffa-taping** Colin the ghoul's leg back in place and was listening to the doctor trying to reason with Mrs Letterman.

Poor Morty was still stuck inside the postbox, and it seemed that Mrs Letterman was refusing to take the **vomiting medicine** the doctor had prescribed.

'But if you'll just take this, Mrs Letterman,' the doctor said, holding up a small bottle of **PUKEITALL**™, 'we can have Morty out of you quicker than a vampire away from a plate of garlic bread!'

'I'm not taking that muck!'
Mrs Letterman protested.
'I swallowed some very
delicate special delivery
packages this morning
and I'm
not insured
against
**vomit
damage.** I'm
very sorry, Doctor,
but Morty will just
have to wait and let
nature take its
course at
the 5.30
postal drop.'

Morty's muffled voice from inside Mrs
Letterman added, '**Don't worry,** Doc. It's nice and
cosy in here, and I've got plenty to read.'

The doctor rolled her eyes several times, **like a
fruit machine coming to a stop,** then turned to
me and said wearily, 'Right, Nurse Ozzy.
Who's left?'

I pointed to the tangled mess that was Delores and Vlad, and the doctor sighed. The sports-maddened pair had crashed into each other with such violence that the receptionist's first, third, fifth, seventh and eighth tentacles were now hideously tangled up with Vlad.

Even worse, they were bickering non-stop with each other.

'Ze **FANGTOMS** ver vinning!' Vlad was insisting. 'You crashed into us becoz you ver about to *looz!* You Oll-Stars are just *sore loozers!'*

'Did my tackle rattle your undead brains?' growled Dolores. 'You weren't winning! As you know, you **vile vampire,** there is only one goal in **MONSTERBALL,** and you have to **SCORE** the goal to win. And your useless team had about as much chance of scoring the goal as Ozzy does of winning this year's **Mr Monsterverse** with legs like those.'

"THE goal?' I asked, ignoring the comment about my legs. 'Aren't there lots of goals in a **MONSTERBALL** game?'

Both monsters stopped **bickering** for a moment and stared at me in **disbelief.**

This happens to me a lot in the monster world.

Vlad laughed. 'Zere is only one net in **MONSTERBALL.** And whichever team puts the monster ball into ze net is ze vinner. Then ze game iz over. Those are ze rules.'

'RULES!' snorted Dolores. 'Suddenly you're an expert on the rules? Your team tried that

outrageously illegal move with the parking meter and the space-hopper outside the **Ghoul boutique!**' One of her free-ish tentacles snaked across the surgery, opened a drawer on her desk and pulled out what seemed to be a small cube. She waved it in Vlad's face. **'Show me where it says that move was legal!'**

I realized that the little cube she was holding was actually a tiny – but very thick – book.

'Pfffft!' Vlad snorted dismissively through his two sharp front teeth. 'It iz in zere somewhere. Maybe in ze sub-section about use of inflatables.'

'HA!' cried Delores triumphantly. 'You know it was a **foul,** which means that the **ALL-STARS** were winning!' She started chanting, **'AWFUL ALL-STARS! AWFUL ALL-STARS!'**

'VANGTOMS VOREVER! VANGTOMS VOREVER!' Vlad snarled, baring an entirely new set of teeth that I hadn't seen before.

'Look at them,' sighed the doctor, shaking her mane of hedge hair. **'Perfectly decent monsters reduced to unthinking savagery in the name of their stupid team!** Mark my words, Ozzy, until there is a cure for team sports, avoid **MONSTERBALL** like the **pustulant plague** it is. We're going to need to keep these two apart before they eat each other. Pass me two medium-sized **monster muzzles,** a **king-size jar of tentacle salve and half a dozen extra-strong T-clamps.'**

It was relatively easy to get a muzzle on Vlad since he's so polite. Delores, however, was altogether more challenging. The doctor and I got there in the end, but at the cost of three pieces of broken office furniture, a shattered picture frame of **Ziggy** and two large dents in the filing cabinet: one doctor-shaped and the other Ozzy-shaped.

'There!' the doctor said finally, wiping her forehead. 'They'll calm down once their stupid Cup Final is finally over this afternoon. Now let's get them separated.'

The doctor showed me how to smear the **tentacle salve generously around the more stubborn knots.** Then, after pointing out the best (and least painful) places to attach the clamps and setting up the electric winch, I remembered Delores's rule book.

'Is it true that no one can understand the **MONSTERBALL** rule book?' I asked.

'Do try to concentrate, Nurse Ozzy!' the monster doctor chided. 'Grab hold of that tentacle. Now, on three. One . . . two . . . three . . . *PUUULLLLLL!*'

With a loud **PLOOOP!** and a painful-sounding **CRACKKK!** Delores and Vlad came apart.

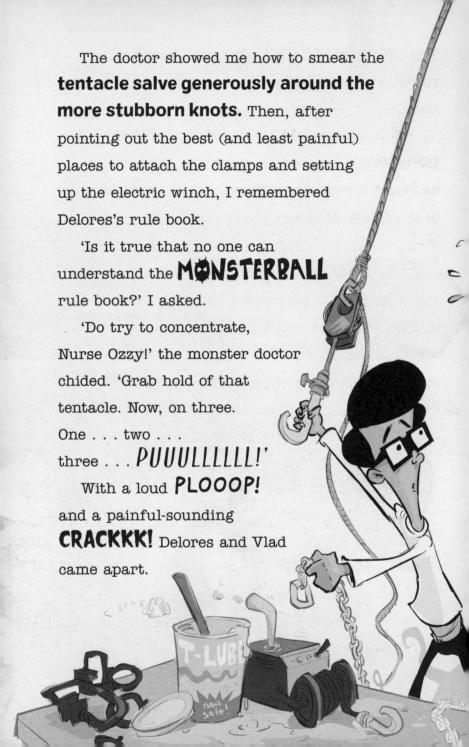

The cube-shaped book went flying from the
receptionist's tentacle. The doctor caught it in one
hand.

**'Of course no one has ever read this
nonsense!'** she scoffed, wiping excess tentacle
salve off the book and flicking it all over the front
of the filing cabinet.

'But why not?' I said.

'Because,' the doctor explained, 'the **MONSTERBALL** rule book is the most *completely ridiculous, nonsensical and contradictory thing ever.* It makes even less sense than a *human perfume commercial.* Here!' she said, tossing the little book to me. 'See for yourself.'

The small book had a logo on the front that looked like either an **angry beachball** or a very round porcupine.

The doctor carefully **un-muzzled** Delores and Vlad. And as the receptionist slithered back into her booth, still glaring angrily at Vlad as he left the surgery, I opened the rule book and began to read.

OFFICIAL
MONSTERBALL RULES
2987th edition

Compiled by the
COMMITTEE to HELP ELIMINATE
ALL TRICKERY in SPORTS
(C.H.E.A.T.S.)

MONSTERBALL

SECTION 1. THE BASICS

(WARNING! Please be aware that all MONSTERBALL rules are strictly enforced by the Old Gods™ in Dimension 5. They are HUGE MONSTERBALL fans, and will punish any breach of the more serious rules with very accurate bolts of lightning.)

THE MATCH

The game of MONSTERBALL can only begin if the referee can convince a monster ball to play. Since monster balls are almost always hungry, this is usually done by promising the ball the smallest member of the losing team for dinner.

THE REFEREE

The referee must remain completely impartial. They MUST NOT cuddle, fall in love with, marry, or join in communal singing with any of the players. Wings (in the form of a BAT-PACK) will be provided to any referee who cannot fly unaided.

THE PITCH

There is no minimum size for a MONSTERBALL pitch. In fact, smaller monsters can play the tabletop version of the game to avoid fatigue. (See APPENDIX 23.)

RULE 1

The pitch has seven corner refuge holes, but the teams may only lurk in them if:

1. There is an unexpected dragon or **frumious bandersnatch** attack.

2. It begins to rain unpleasant acid sleet.

RULE 2

To avoid confusion there is now only one net in which to score a goal.

The net is usually a Nettteee from Dimension 4.6, but any foul-tasting string-based monster will suffice.

RULE 3

There can only be one goal scored in a MONSTERBALL match, and the match is over when that goal has been scored. The goal is scored when any player 'encourages' the monster ball into the goal. This can be done using any part of the player's anatomy they are prepared to risk losing.

PAMPERED PROFESSIONAL POSERS

Chapter 4

I looked up from the rule book. 'It doesn't sound too bad. No worse than golf.'

'Ha! That's just the first few pages,' said the doctor. 'There's another nine hundred and eighty-three of **nonsense** that have been added over the centuries. **MONSTERBALL** used to be fun in the beginning. Admittedly it never had the *proud* and *ancient pedigree of mammoth racing...*' The doctor got the faraway look in her eyes she always gets whenever she thinks about her favourite extinct sport.

'**Ah! Now there was a sport!**' she sighed. 'The icy pitch! *The thunder of mighty hooves!* The heady cocktail of **skill, danger** and *extreme hairstyling.* The perfect harmony of monster and mammo—'

'Were you ever a fan of **M⊗NSTERBALL?**' I interrupted, quickly changing the subject.

'What? Oh, well, back in the early days, yes!' she admitted. 'There was something entertaining about the sight of monsters in **embarrassingly short shorts** trying to pick up a very **hungry monster ball.** But then came the TV deals, the big money, the agents, the pundits and the celebrity players. And before you could say '*pampered professional posers*' the werewolf players had hair-product contracts and the vampires were advertising tooth-sharpeners. Then the league brought in a *ridiculously complicated rule book* that no one could understand on the grounds of making it "safer". **Which, of course, took all the fun out of it.'**

'But surely every sport needs rules,' I said. 'Even **mammoth racing** must've had some.'

'Of course it did,' she snapped. Then she began to recite, 'Rule 1. Contestants must have a mammoth. *There is no size limit.* Rule 2. At the starting bun, the contestants race towards the finish line—'

'Don't you mean **"starting gun"?'** I interrupted.

'"Starting **GUN?"'** snorted the doctor. 'Why would the referee shoot one of the contestants? You humans have some strange notions of sporting conduct. **No. No. No.** The race begins with the referee firing a *delicious bun* towards the finish line so the mammoths can chase after it.'

I hadn't realized there were any sports that involved *patisserie projectiles.* And I was just having a brilliant idea about how school sports lessons could be made more bearable with the introduction of *salted caramel and chocolate* when the emergency phone rang.

I snatched it up and put on my official medical emergency voice. *'You have reached the monster doctor surgery's emergency medical line. Please state the nature of your monster medical emergency.'*

'You must come **IMMEDIATELY!**' an agitated (and slightly hammy) voice on the line said. 'Before it's **TOO** late.'

'What seems to be the problem?' I asked professionally.

'There's BEEN a Level 1 **DEATH!**' the speaker said rather dramatically.

'I am very sorry to hear that,' I replied sympathetically. 'But wouldn't it be better to call an **undertaker** or a **zombie life-change consultant?**'

For monsters, death isn't always as serious as it tends to be for humans. *There are five different levels of monster death.* The standard definitions of which are as follows.

LEVEL
1

The patient's body is intact enough for resurrection, re-animation or viral un-deadness (i.e. vampirism) by an after life change consultant.

LEVEL 2 The patient is too digested or in too many different pieces/locations/dimensions for any affordable treatment.

LEVEL 3+ Are to do with the Old Gods™ and therefore far too difficult for monsters or humans to understand.

The speaker didn't seem to have heard what I'd said, though. 'Were you *LISTENING* to me? I SAID a Level 1.5 death. **Which means time IS of the ESSENCE!'**

'A Level 1.5 death?' I asked. 'What's that?'

'Oh good GRIEF!' snapped the speaker. 'Who is this? Where's the *REAL* monster doctor? You're *wasting valuable* time when there *MIGHT* still be a chance of getting her back into *PLAY!'*

Before I could say another word, the monster doctor had dived across the room and snatched the phone out of my hand.

'A Level 1.5 death, you say?' she barked into the handset. 'How long ago was the patient eaten?'

She scribbled down **LESS THAN FIVE MINUTES AGO** on a notepad. 'And where exactly are you?' She transcribed a set of inter-dimensional coordinates to the note. Then she hung up, called the **basement garage** and told Lance to meet us outside in thirty seconds. She pushed me through the waiting room and out into Lovecraft Avenue just as Lance, **the big white monster ambulance,** screeched to a halt in front of us.

'Get in,' she said. 'There's not a moment to lose. I'll explain on the way.'

A DIMENSION OF SIGHT AND SOUND

Chapter 5

The doctor **bounced** into Lance's driving seat and clambered up the **pile of cushions** that allowed her to reach the steering wheel.

'**Let's GO!**' she said. 'There's not an **eenie-meenie-micro-second** Ⴟ to be lost! And,' she added confidentially, 'if I hadn't found a reason to get away from those **MONSTERBALL-MAD** monsters **RIGHT NOW** I swear I might have started practising **experimental surgical procedures** on them.'

Inside his little jar on the dashboard Bruce flapped his wings irritably. Glowing letters appeared on his communication screen.

WHERE ARE WE GOING?

I held up the paper with the scribbled
coordinates.

THAT'S UPSIDE-DOWN.
DUMMY.

'Surely you're the one that's upside down?' I
said, tired of Bruce's rudeness to me.

Monster ambulances (like our lovely Lance)
are born able to travel between the six dimensions
at will, but as they have a **terrible** sense of
direction, they usually take a BAT-NAV with

42

them. Lance's BAT-NAV is called Bruce, and due to a manufacturing fault he is **very, very rude.**

Especially to me.

'Ha! Well said, Ozzy!' The doctor laughed. 'It's about time you stood up to little **Mr Grumpy Ears.'**

Bruce squeaked what was no doubt some incredibly high-pitched insult at me.

'Ozzy can't help the position of his hair, Bruce,' chided the doctor. *'Apologize at once!'*

Bruce squeaked pathetically, like a mouse with a chest complaint.

'That's better,' said the doctor. 'Now, if you can get us to the coordinates in the next five minutes, there might be a packet of *Belgian chocolate coated blue-bottles* in it for you.'

I immediately felt Lance's inter-dimensional engine *THRUMMMMMMM* into action. We zoomed off down Lovecraft Avenue, gathering speed as we went, and just before we crashed through the window of the new *horn waxing parlour* Lance turned backthwards and spun forward thricewards. As I tried not to throw up my breakfast, we slipped out of Dimension 3.142 and into . . .

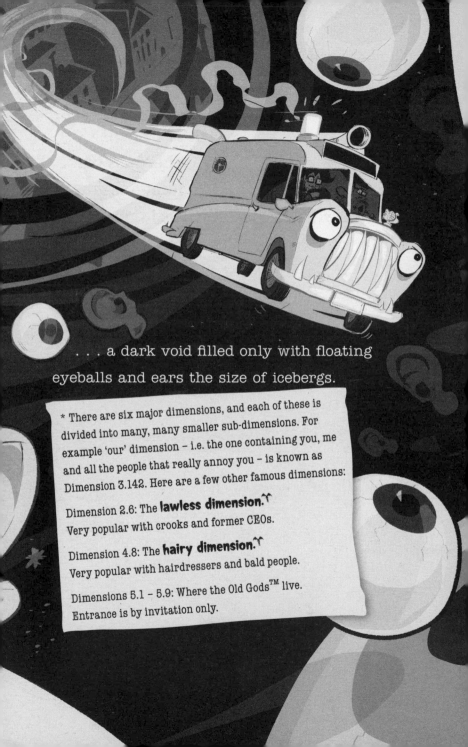

. . . a dark void filled only with floating eyeballs and ears the size of icebergs.

* There are six major dimensions, and each of these is divided into many, many smaller sub-dimensions. For example 'our' dimension – i.e. the one containing you, me and all the people that really annoy you – is known as Dimension 3.142. Here are a few other famous dimensions:

Dimension 2.6: The **lawless dimension.**🐦
Very popular with crooks and former CEOs.

Dimension 4.8: The **hairy dimension.**🐦
Very popular with hairdressers and bald people.

Dimensions 5.1 – 5.9: Where the Old Gods™ live.
Entrance is by invitation only.

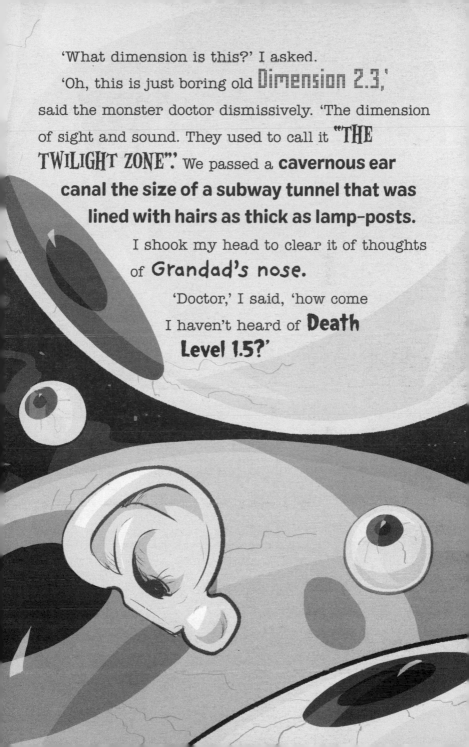

'What dimension is this?' I asked.

'Oh, this is just boring old Dimension 2.3,' said the monster doctor dismissively. 'The dimension of sight and sound. They used to call it "THE TWILIGHT ZONE".' We passed a **cavernous ear canal the size of a subway tunnel that was lined with hairs as thick as lamp-posts.**

I shook my head to clear it of thoughts of **Grandad's nose.**

'Doctor,' I said, 'how come I haven't heard of **Death Level 1.5?'**

'Well, the research is still quite new,' the doctor admitted. *'Only a few centuries old.'* Outside Lance's windscreen, **a planet-sized monster eyeball** lazily followed us orbit past it. 'A few hundred years ago the A&E department at *St. Undertakers Hospital* began investigating patients who had been involved in A.T.E. episodes.'

'A.T.E.?' I asked. **'Accidental Temper Eating,'** she explained. 'You know the kind of thing: a married couple having a **heated argument about** an improperly

flushed toilet, **school monsterlings** hurling insults about the **lack of drool** at the edge of your mouth. **Tempers fray and, before you know it, somebody has been eaten.** Then it's all tears and, **"Oh! I'm so sorry! I didn't mean to eat you!"** and you're on the way to the A&E department. Let's face it, it's happened to us all.'

I didn't tell her that as bad as my school was no one had ever been eaten in an argument. (Yet.)

'Anyway, **Dr Coffyn-Dodger** and his team realized that at least 50% of Level 2 deaths could be prevented **if the eaten patient was extracted before the eater's stomach juices got going**. It was revolutionary work!'

'So a Level 1.5 death indicates that a patient has been eaten, but might still survive?' I asked.

The doctor nodded.

'That's amazing!' I said. 'So who has been eaten?'

The doctor shook her head. 'I don't know.' She turned to the BAT-NAV. 'Where are we heading Bruce?'

Bruce began to giggle. He sounded like a mouse that has been inhaling helium.

'And what exactly is SO funny?' demanded the doctor.

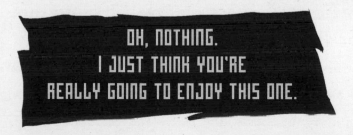

OH, NOTHING.
I JUST THINK YOU'RE
REALLY GOING TO ENJOY THIS ONE.

Before
the doctor
could ask what
he meant, Bruce said:

**HOLD ON.
WE'RE ALMOST THERE.**

Lance dived straight into the ear
canal of one of the giant floating ears.
Everything instantly went **dark, hairy** and
waxy.

With a familiar **stomach-flipping bungee
lurch** we hurtled into another dimension and
found ourselves in a lovely cloudy green sky, about
a thousand feet up and **falling rapidly** towards
the ground.

Once upon a time that might have worried me. (The falling, I mean, not the green sky. That's perfectly normal.) But Lance is extremely good at things like not crashing into the ground and **exploding** in a fireball.

So instead I occupied myself by wondering what the blue ring down below was. It looked a bit like a park (monster grass is usually blue or purple). There were a few small areas of water, and some things that might have been trees dotted about here and there. But as we **plummeted** closer to the ground, I saw a rather odd – and very thick – wall around the park.

I was about to ask the doctor what it was when I realized she had gone that *peculiar shade of pale blue* that means she's had an **awful shock.**

'**Oh no!**' she groaned, pointing to a strange pattern of white lines that criss-crossed the grass. 'It can't be, can it? **And not today of all days?**'

Bruce sniggered again.

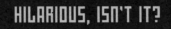

HILARIOUS, ISN'T IT?

Just before we crashed into the ground, Lance *swooped* in a way that briefly reminded my mouth what it had eaten for breakfast. Then we landed gently on a patch of the *luxurious blue turf,* and Lance trundled to a stop beside a brightly coloured corner flag that said:

**MONSTERBALL
CUP FINAL**
SPONSORED BY BADIDAS

The doctor put her head in her hands.
Bruce's screen lit up.

**WELCOME TO
THE MONSTERBALL
CUP FINAL, DOC!**

SAFETY INNOVATIONS

Chapter 6

The **MONSTERBALL** pitch seemed to be *completely empty.*

Where were the stands packed with **screaming** and *slavering* **ALL-STAR** and **FANGTOM** spectators? The pitch was surrounded by nothing more exciting than a tall, thick glass screen with **flickering** **adverts** for the latest **electric Toe-Shaver.**

'Where are all the supporters?' I asked as we exited Lance.

The doctor pulled herself together and waved one hand dismissively at the large screen.

'**Behind their precious safety glass,**' she tutted disapprovingly. 'Yet another of those **new-fangled "safety innovations"** I mentioned.' She **harrumphed.**

'All nonsense, of course. The risk of being eaten is half the fun of attending a sporting event!'

She shook her head sadly and looked around. 'So where is our patient?'

'Those must be the players,' I said, pointing to a **clump of monsters** milling around two small buildings that I assumed were the team dugouts.

'EXCUUUUUUUUUUUUSE ME!'

bellowed the doctor to the group as she hurried towards them.

'WHICH ONE OF YOU CALLED FOR A MONSTER
DOCTOR?' I hurried off after her, but had barely
got more than fifty feet when something barred
my way, **flapping annoyingly** right in my face.
'REFRESHMENTS!'
it screeched, sounding
like a market
trader whose
voice hasn't
broken yet. A
small winged
monster with
**one staring
eye** started shoving
a tray in my face. 'GET YOUR CROAK-A-COLA,
LICE CREAM AND SPECIAL SOUVENIR MATCH
PROGRAMMES HERE!'

It darted left and right, blocking my attempts to
get past it. 'Player biographies and glossy pictures.
All the latest match news! GO ON! ONLY ONE
KARLOFF! GO ON! ONLY ONE KARLOFF! GO ON!
ONLY ONE KAR—'

I had to buy one in the end just to get the annoying thing to go away.

Up close the team dugouts were more like **military bunkers.** All concrete and bullet-proof glass. The **ALL-STAR** and **FANGTOM** players were gathered together in a group, talking nervously and shivering in their *extremely short shorts.*

'Where's the patient?' the doctor snapped at them as I arrived.

I was surprised to see a **spectacularly handsome werewolf** lope towards us. Most werewolves are dreadfully **scruffy** and **smell terrible** because they're always rolling in **revolting** things they've found on the moors. But this one looked as if he'd just strolled out of the pet-grooming parlour. **He ran one long manicured paw through his enormous bouffant hair** whilst the other tapped impatiently on the furry case of his smartphone.

According to the player profiles in my programme, this was the famous Vulfgang Werewolf.

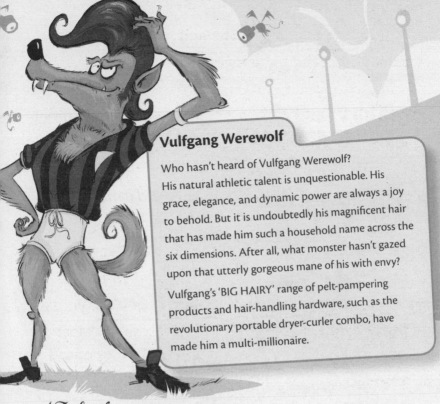

Vulfgang Werewolf

Who hasn't heard of Vulfgang Werewolf? His natural athletic talent is unquestionable. His grace, elegance, and dynamic power are always a joy to behold. But it is undoubtedly his magnificent hair that has made him such a household name across the six dimensions. After all, what monster hasn't gazed upon that utterly gorgeous mane of his with envy?

Vulfgang's 'BIG HAIRY' range of pelt-pampering products and hair-handling hardware, such as the revolutionary portable dryer-curler combo, have made him a multi-millionaire.

'*At last!*' Vulfgang said in the same overly theatrical accent of our emergency caller. 'You simply **MUST** get her back! It is essential that the match starts at once. The situation is **QUITE** ridiculous! Even the managers haven't seen anything like it before.' He pointed to the dugouts where the **ALL-STARS** manager – an enormous red-faced troll in a shabby **ALL-STARS** tracksuit – was **sobbing uncontrollably** whilst gnawing splinters out of the team's oak bench.

In the **FANGTOMS** dugout, the vampire manager was so angry they kept flipping back and forth to their bat-form, and **banging into the bulletproof glass windows like a confused fly.**

The doctor and I were looking around, but there didn't seem to be any obvious signs of an eaten patient anywhere. There were no unattended limbs or tentacles on the ground.

'Where is our patient?' the doctor repeated from between tightly clenched teeth.

'You said someone has been eaten?' I reminded the werewolf. 'Level 1.5 death? Rather urgent?'

'THERE, of course!' said Vulfgang, as if it were completely obvious. He was pointing to a spherical object on the pitch that I hadn't noticed earlier, because it was exactly the same shade of blue as the grass. But on closer examination I could now see that the spherical object was actually a monster. It was a bit like a space-hopper with spikes and huge teeth, and it was frowning grumpily.

The doctor looked annoyed. 'That's just an ordinary monster ball,' she scoffed. 'HOW can a monster ball be my patient?'

'The monster ball isn't the PATIENT!' said Vulfgang frustratedly. 'The patient is INSIDE the monster ball!'

The doctor muttered something angrily under her breath. I only managed to catch the words, 'monsterball', 'stupid', 'game' and 'mammoth' before she began to turn that particular shade of blue that means she is about to either:

a. **Explode with fury.**
b. **Do that horrible screamy-thing that makes all the mugs in the kitchen shatter at once.**

'Do you mean to tell me that you called my emergency line to report that a monster ball has eaten a monster at a **MONSTERBALL** match?' Her right eyelid was beginning to throb alarmingly.

I stepped back.

'But there are complications you don't underst—' began Vulfgang.

But the doctor had had enough.

'WHAT A COMPLETE WASTE OF OUR TIME!' she exploded. 'Monster balls are **SUPPOSED** to eat the players! **That's the whole point of your stupid game!'** She turned and started stomping off across the pitch, back to where Lance was parked. 'Come on, Ozzy! If we get back to the surgery in time for afternoon *coughee* there might be some *salted caramel muckaroons* left.'

'But what should we do?' Vulfgang called anxiously after us.

'Just start your silly match, of course!' the doctor yelled.

But that's the problem!' exclaimed Vulfgang. 'We can't!'

The doctor stopped.

'Why, in the name of my **never-ending nostril hair,** not?' she asked.

'Because only the referee can start a **MONSTERBALL** match. And **OUR** referee is the one—' he pointed to the monster ball again — 'that the monster ball ate!'

THAT'S A STUPID RULE!

Chapter 7

A second player hopped forward. (Literally. His entire body was poking out of the top of what was definitely a single giant football boot.)

Toeknee Stomper

Solid, steady and down-to-earth, the ALL-STARS striker has always had a simple attitude to the game of MONSTERBALL. 'I just kick things,' he says with typical modesty. He's a player of few words, choosing instead to let his foot do the talking.

Off the pitch Toeknee's hobbies include hop-scotch (in which he is semi-professional), pedicures and long hops in the country.

'Stop being so rude, Wulfie!' said the monster cheerfully, holding out a tiny hand. 'Toeknee Stomper's the name! And, blimey, are we pleased to see you, Doc! The problem started when the ref got into a bit of a **barney** with the monster ball,' continued Toeknee. 'The daft object has been in a **shocking mood** since it rolled up this morning! It wouldn't let the ref start the match. **So she lost her temper and told the ball to shut up and play.** Well, that tore it! The ball rolled off for a *sulk* in corner refuge No.3 over there.'

DISPUTE AT FINAL! ◀◀ REPLAY

I was starting to see why the monster doctor liked mammoth racing so much. It sounded lovely and straightforward by comparison.

Toeknee continued. 'So that gave the ref the right **hump,** I can tell you. And, on top of that, all the players were shouting at her and the **ALL-STARS** manager had already begun **eating the furniture.** So the ref invoked Rule 1.'

RULE 1

The pitch has seven corner refuge holes, but the teams may only lurk in them if:

1. There is an unexpected dragon or **frumious bandersnatch** attack.

2. It begins to rain unpleasant acid sleet.

I remembered that one from earlier.

'But the monster ball wasn't having any of that,' said Toeknee. 'It said Rule 1 didn't apply to monster balls because they're not on any **TEAM,** and **it blew a raspberry at the referee.** So what with that – and the crowd starting to **sing rude songs about the ref's antennae** – I reckon she just lost her temper and **kicked** the monster ball.'

The doctor looked horrified. **Her eyes gaped wide. As did her mouth, nostrils and even her earholes.**

'Complete madness, I know!' agreed Toeknee gesturing around at his monstrous fellow players. 'I mean, we're all **trained professionals** and it's still dangerous enough for us! **But a civilian kicking a monster ball?** Madness.'

'How long ago **EXACTLY** was the patient eaten?' asked the doctor quickly.

'About fifteen minutes,' replied Toeknee.

'RIGHT, OZZY!' said the doctor. 'Taking into account the **tremendous** power of a monster ball's digestive juices I reckon we have about ten minutes to get her out.'

'How are you going to do it?' I asked. **'Explosives? Dissection? A tow rope attached to Lance?** Just so you know, **I'm not climbing down a monster's throat again.'**

'No, no, no,' reassured the doctor. 'I'm just going to try your **revolutionary** technique of talking – very politely – to **an incredibly dangerous patient.'**

One head of a huge man-eating plant burst out laughing. It was wearing the **FANGTOMS** strip.

'So you're just going to say, *"Dear monster ball, please can we have our referee back?"* the head (I think it was Violet) sneered. **'That's ridiculous.'**

'Possibly,' said the doctor. 'But I can assure you that my assistant Ozzy – despite his **primitive** ape-like brain and body – has had remarkable success with this very technique.'

'Primitive?' I echoed.

'Primitive in the most positive way!' the doctor said cheerfully, patting me on the head as if I were a particularly bright and helpful Border collie. She turned back to the players. 'Since he began working for me he has managed to solve

all sorts of tricky problems.
Often without resorting to
shouting,
biting or
setting
fire to any
of our patients!'
She announced
this as if it were
something to be
rather proud of.
The rest
of the players
looked at me
sceptically.
They clearly
weren't a crowd
used to sorting

things out without resorting to
shouting, biting or setting them on fire.

The doctor ignored their unimpressed stares
and strode confidently over to the monster ball.

'Hello, monster ball!' she said. 'How are you
today?'

The monster ball glared up at her, its **huge teeth** *glistening in the sun.* Then it opened its mouth **VERY** wide, baring **row upon row of spiky fangs.**

'ARE YOU SERIOUS?'

Chapter 8

The monster ball's tooth-packed mouth closed as snug and tight as a very expensive bank vault. 'How am I feeling?' it growled. 'I'll tell you how I'm feeling! Thoroughly fed-up and tired!' It yawned, revealing the pink tunnel down which the referee had disappeared. 'I was up till half past three last night! The Dimension 2 play-off game between the **Thunder Lizards** and the **Grrrrrlly Growlers** went on and on and on and on. Thought I'd never get to bed what with all the endless **stupid nit-picking** about the rules. I was so sick of it all this morning, and then the referee starts having a go at me and . . .' It licked its lips and perked up a bit. 'But at least I got to eat a referee. So I suppose things are looking up.'

The doctor nodded as if this were a perfectly normal sort of thing to hear in a conversation. 'Was there any particular reason why you ate the referee?' she asked. **'I don't mean to judge, of course.** I mean who hasn't wanted to eat a referee at some time or other?' She gave a **hearty laugh.**

'I'm a monster ball . . .' replied the monster ball, as if the doctor were a bit dim. **'Eating monsters is what we do.'**

'Of course it is. **Absolutely!** And eating **MONSTERBALL** players is good, clean fun,' the doctor said sympathetically. But then she pretended to think for a moment, before adding, 'And I'm sure you've read all the latest warnings about the dangers of eating a referee's **new toxic strip?'**

The monster ball looked momentarily puzzled. 'Toxic?' it said. 'I've never heard of toxic strips!'

'Really?' asked the doctor *as innocently as my baby sister filling her nappy.* 'It's nothing to worry about. Just another one of those **silly new safety features.'** She rolled her eyes. 'Referees now wear toxic shorts to prevent them from being eaten. Ridiculous if you ask me. **Health and safety gone mad.'**

The monster ball now looked a little *concerned.* 'Are the TOXIC . . . are they dangerous to monster balls?'

'Of course not!' snorted the doctor. 'Everyone knows you monster balls are indestructible. I suppose it might make you feel a bit **vomity** for a while.

But not for more than a century or two. Then you'll be right as rain – apart from the **lingering side-effects,** that is.' She turned to me and winked. 'Nurse Ozzy, remind me what the most severe side-effects of referee poisoning are?'

I pretended to recite from memory. 'Nothing worse than severe **volcano tummy, high-speed running bottom** and, in some of the more serious cases, **earwax moustaches.'**

The monster ball began unconsciously biting its nails. 'Surely there must be some kind of cure?' A note of concern was creeping into its voice.

'Of course there is!' said the doctor. 'You can just **vomit** up the referee.'

The monster ball now looked even more worried.

'But monster balls can't vomit!' it cried. A note of panic was sharply elbowing the concern out of its voice. **'When we monster balls eat something it's supposed to stay good and eaten!'**

'I hadn't thought of that!' exclaimed the doctor. 'I'd love to help you but I haven't got any—' she began to absentmindedly pat her various jacket pockets. **'AH-HA!'** she exclaimed. 'Yes, I do!' And she produced the small bottle of **PUKEITALL** that Mrs Letterman had refused back at the surgery. **'You're in luck.** This stuff will soon sort you out.'

PUKEITALL

Consumed with regret after consuming someone?

Then take – new improved – PUKEITALL!

Guaranteed to make you vomit within 30 seconds!

REMEMBER: DON'T DELAY – PUKE TODAY!

WARNING May contain nuts (or bolts). The manufacturers cannot be held responsible for property damage incurred by violent projectile vomiting.)

Without giving the monster ball any time to think, the doctor said in a loud commanding voice, **'OPEN WIDE!'** Then she poured the entire contents of the bottle down the monster ball's throat.

When the bottle was empty the monster ball said, 'Hmmm . . . An interesting taste. **Reminds me of a troll's underpants I ate back in 1795.** Are you sure this stuff will work on me? We monster balls are pretty toug—'

But the rest of its words were drowned out by the **biggest, squelchiest, most disgusting belch I've ever heard outside of a school changing room.**

The monster ball's mouth opened impossibly wide and it began **barfing** something out on to the pitch. It was like watching a cat **regurgitate** a furball far, far bigger than the actual cat.

It was **fascinatingly disgusting.**

Once it was over, there was an **insect monster** about the same size as a Great Dane lying on the pitch. It was wearing a very damp black-and-white-striped referee's strip, and was soaked in some **gooey purple stuff** that looked an awful lot like cheap supermarket shower gel.

'Are you alright?' I asked the referee.

'Of course I cheesecaked!' said the referee, her antennae waving around in the air like my dad's arms when he's listening to music. 'But would someone kindly park my elephant **inside** the parachute hangar?'

'Pardon?' I said. I didn't quite follow the odd direction the conversation had suddenly taken.

'The iceberg, of course!' snapped the referee impatiently, as if I were the one not making any sense. 'It has been sitting on my **blancmange helicopter** and the **peach anthrax will never clean off the upholstery!'**

The doctor and I looked at each other. 'Symptoms, Nurse Ozzy?' she asked.

'Um . . . surrealistic speech patterns,' I said. Then, peering closer, I added, **'Dancing eyeballs and, er . . . wandering antennae?'**

'Well done! Which put together mean . . . ?' the doctor probed.

I looked at her blankly. She sighed. 'Did you not notice the **counter-clockwise leg wobbling?'** she asked crossly. 'Which is always a dead giveaway for . . .?'

'**Of COURSE!**' I cried. '**They are all classic symptoms of arthropod concussion.**'

'Well done, Nurse Ozzy!' she said, then turned to the approaching players. '**I'm afraid that this referee is broken.** There is no way the Cup Final can continue.'

But the referee disagreed. She staggered upright and shook the doctor and me off. 'Take your **filthy leg-warmers** off me!' she demanded. 'I'm as fit as a f—' But we never got to find out exactly what she was as fit as because she collapsed face first on to the pitch and began to **snore** loudly.

'Oh, wonderful!' said Vulfgang in an annoyingly sarcastic tone that wasn't at all helpful. 'Now we've got NO referee at all!'

I looked around the stadium. There were tens of thousands of spectators out there behind the glass.

'Surely there's at least **one** monster out there who could referee the **MONSTERBALL** final,' I said, pointing to the unseen crowd.

The players all **snorted, snuffled, burped and screeched** with laughter.

The doctor shook her head. 'You've as much chance of finding an impartial monster in this crowd as you have of finding a *vegetarian vampire*.'

'It can't be THAT hard,' I said. **'All they need is someone trustworthy and either completely fearless or completely stupid,** who has absolutely no vested interest whatsoever in which team of monsters wins this game. Someone who—' I stopped talking. The doctor was staring at me oddly. And so were all the players.

I recognized the look on their faces. It was the same one my family has when the takeaway pizza finally arrives.

I realized what they were all thinking.

'No,' I said quickly. 'I can't do it. I won't do it. I . . . I . . . I don't even know any of the rules of **MONSTERBALL!** And in any case –' I desperately racked my brain for an excuse – '**I don't have any shorts!**'

But the doctor was bent over the unconscious referee. 'Humans might not be monstrous enough to actually play **MONSTERBALL,** but there's nothing stopping them from refereeing.' She yanked something off the ref's lower half and straightened up, holding a **damp and gooey garment that reminded me of my dog Piglet's chew blanket.**

She handed it to me.

'What were you saying about not having any shorts?'

AVOID THE PIRANHAS

Chapter 9

There are moments when I find the **sensible part of my brain watching in horror** as a different part of my consciousness and my body join hands and go **waltzing off together into the sunset, to do something I'd really much rather they didn't.**

It seems to be happening a lot more since I became an apprentice to the monster doctor. Which might explain why, ten minutes later, I was standing in the middle of the pitch with a *whiztle* in my mouth, about to referee the **MONSTERBALL** Cup Final.

And on top of that I was wearing somebody else's shorts.

I hate shorts – even when they're mine they make me look like a **disappointed heron** – and these belonged to the referee and therefore had one more leg than was **entirely normal** for a human. The doctor had done the best she could with a needle and zombie stitching thread, but as I stood there with Toeknee Stomper strapping me into the referee's spare **BAT-PACK,** the shorts were chafing terribly.

RULE 14B

As the game of MONSTERBALL takes place (mostly) in three dimensions, it is necessary for the referee to fly. If the referee cannot fly unaided, or is too lazy, a telepathic **BAT-PACK** will be provided free of charge by the match organizers.

(Please remember to return your **BAT-PACK** in the condition in which it was provided. **BAT-PACK** will not operate underwater and are only fire-proof up to 800 degrees F.)

'Don't worry!

There's nothing to it!' shouted the doctor from the sideline.

'The **BAT-PACK** will just read your mind and take you wherever you want to go. You've got a copy of the rule book and absolutely no bias for either team, **so you're already more qualified than most monster referees!** Just remember: be firm but fair, avoid the **frumious bandersnatch** if it shows up, and **try not to get incinerated, eaten by piranhas or catapulted into another sub-dimension.** And don't touch anything – especially the monster ball!'

With those helpful words ringing in my ears, I blew the *whiztle* and started the match.

The **ALL-STARS** kicked off. Toeknee Stomper hopped up and with his **enormous boot** sent the monster ball *soaring* in an arc high across the pitch. I only had to think about it and the **BAT-PACK** flapped me up into the air, automatically following the play. It felt amazing! I was actually flying (again). **And this time I hadn't had to be vomited out of a dragon to do it.**

Even better, the telepathic **BAT-PACK** meant I was now free to concentrate on the **insanely weird task** of refereeing a **M◆NSTERBALL** Cup Final.

'BLIMEY!' said the monster ball as I pulled alongside it. 'That Toeknee Stomper's got a heck of a foot on him!' Then it laughed, overcome with the sheer delight of flying. **'HAHAHAHA!** This is more like it!' It turned and yelled, **'COME AND GET ME, YOU FLAPPY FIENDS!'** This comment was directed at the 'wingers', who were now frantically flapping in pursuit of the monster ball.

A 'winger' in **M◆NSTERBALL** is a player who can fly. Their job is to use any kind of a bat (the 'hitty' version rather than the 'flappy' version) to **whack** the monster ball back down to the pitch if it gets **kicked, punched, thrown, or catapulted above head height.** The **ALL-STARS** winger – an **annoying** little insecty thing called the Buzz-Bomber – reached the monster ball first.

THWACKKK

Buzz-Bomber

It's easy to see why the ALL-STARS' Buzz-Bomber has received the MONSTERBALL league's 'Most Irritating Player' award for the last three seasons. The combination of her annoying voice and parasitic personality allows her to get right under the skin of her opponents. But her aggressive antics make her very popular with the younger monsters. And sales of her trademark bats – the Zinger Stinger – remain huge.

I kept well out of the way as the Buzz-Bomber gave the monster ball an almighty **THWACKKK** and sent it zipping back down to the pitch like a falling meteor. Her teammate, Krakatoer, saw it coming and blew her top.

Literally.

An eruption of molten lava exploded out of the top of her head, and neatly caught the monster ball in mid-air.

'HOO-HOO! HAHAHAHA! That tickles!' sniggered the monster ball as it **balanced on top of the column of burning lava.** Then, in an incredible display of **lava-juggling** skill, Krakatoer slithered off, carrying the monster ball towards where the single goal waited on the edge of the pitch. I followed as close behind as I could without suffering **third-degree burns** –

though my eyebrows did get a bit **singed.** None of the **FANGTOWN** players were stupid enough to try to tackle the **molten marvel.** One by one, they backed away, leaving only their defender, Twiggy the tree-monster, in the way.

Twiggy

The position of defender in the ALL-STARS team only became available when their previous defender, Rocky Range, was injured after he suffered a massive landslide. Luckily for the ALL-STARS, Twiggy had recently been exiled from the forest kingdom of Woodonia for a rude comment she'd made about the king's severe pruning policy.

Her decision to branch out into MONSTERBALL has grown into a permanent position with the ALL-STARS, and she has really begun to put down roots at the club.

Twiggy had rather unwisely planted herself slap bang in front of the goal, but was now hurriedly uprooting as the lava monster's **fiery form** approached. Like most trees, she wasn't a huge fan of fire. It seemed as though nothing could stop Krakatoer from scoring – the final would be over almost before it had begun! With no one *(especially me)* injured.

I got ready to blow my *whiztle* for a goal, but I had barely touched it to my lips when Krakatoer stepped on a **booby-square.**

Hurrah!

This **booby-square** concealed a **big spring-in-a-box.** In an instant, Krakatoer and the monster ball were

BOIIIINNNNGGGEDDDDDD

five hundred feet above the pitch, the huge spring wobbling back and forth below them. Before she could react, the Bat-in-the-Hat had flapped into action.

Extract from

OWWW! THAT HURT!

A guide to MONSTERBALL and Other Monster Sports

MONSTERBALL

BOOBY-SQUARES

Booby-squares are a unique feature of professional **MONSTERBALL**. Before the match, and in great secrecy, the match organizers booby-trap the pitch with two dozen randomly located booby-squares. When stepped on, these instantly trigger a penalty.

Popular penalties include:

Dropping the player into a completely different sub-dimension. Dimension 3.9 is very popular and safe as it is mostly made of jelly and has a very good taxi service.

Covering the player in ultra-quick drying cement.

Piranha tanks – or in some more brutal games, deep-sea denture devils.

The ever popular big spring-in-a-box square.

The Bat-in-the-Hat

The Bat-in-the-Hat is a vampire known as much for his crazy headgear as his eccentric playing style. Early in his career he favoured enormous cowboy hats, sombreros and even – on one memorable occasion – an entire living-hedge hat. But in recent years he's chosen the more mature and elegant formality of Victorian toppers or horned Viking helmets.

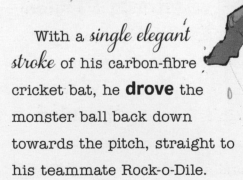

With a *single elegant stroke* of his carbon-fibre cricket bat, he **drove** the monster ball back down towards the pitch, straight to his teammate Rock-o-Dile.

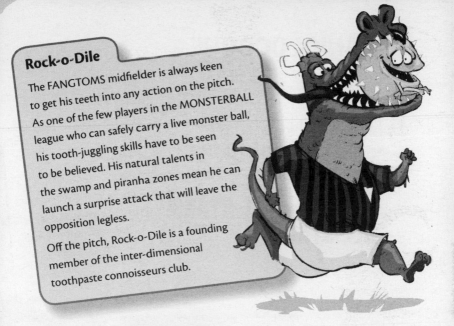

I willed the **BAT-PACK** to dive me down to pitch level in pursuit of the action. To my amazement, Rock-o simply **opened his jaws wide and neatly caught the ball in his teeth.** This looked **terribly dangerous** – after all, the monster ball can eat almost any monster (apart from the goal, which is apparently too **stringy** and **fiddly** to bother eating). But Rock-o-Dile had the ball's teeth facing outwards so it couldn't eat him.

As Rock-o-Dile scurried towards the goal, I was flying close enough to hear the **thwarted monster ball** giving Rock-o a compliment.

'**Very clever!**' it said admiringly. 'Nicely done.'

'**AANKK OOOOH!**' said Rock-o-Dile as he raced off towards the goal with his head thrown back and his tongue **flapping out behind him like a scarf.**

'**COME ON, ROCK-O!**' cried the **FANGTOM** supporters.

'**SCRAG HIM, ALL-STARS!**' cried the **ALL-STARS** fans.

But, unfortunately, Rock-o's long, upturned snout meant he couldn't see directly ahead of him.

Which is why he ran flat-out into a wall.

HIS HAIR WAS PERFECT

Chapter 10

It wasn't actually a wall, of course.
It was the Stenchman.

The Stenchman

Whiffy Trenchfoot was born beneath the bridge at Whiffy's Crossing and was all set to follow a career in the family toll business when he was bitten by a zombie.

However, all was not lost. When Wiffy was resurrected, he discovered he had an amazing talent for MONSTERBALL. His complete immunity to damage, enormous feet (size 87!) and overpoweringly horrendous smell have made him an indispensable member of the ALL-STARS team for the last 77 seasons.

But running into a **nine foot tall, thirty stone zombie-troll** is pretty much the same as running into a wall. **Only harder. And smellier.**

Luckily, my **BAT-PACK** had spotted the Stenchman and just managed to *swoop* us both over the top. But Rock-o-Dile crashed into him so hard that the impact **popped** the monster ball clean out of his jaws. The ball bounced across the blue grass of the pitch, with the Stenchman *frantically lumbering after it, as nimbly as an elephant with all four legs in plaster.*

But he never caught it.

The **FANGTOM'S** cool thinking ice-man, 'the Bergman', opened his craggy white mouth and belched out a force-five gale of frozen snow and ice.

The Bergman

The eccentric fridge and freezer magnet, Brandon Smegg, was turned into an I.T. (Iced Thing) when his experimental ice cream reactor melted down. But luckily Smegg quickly realized that his new ice-wielding abilities and chilled-out attitude would lend themselves to a career in MONSTERBALL.

Now, when things begin to heat up on the pitch, the FANGTOMS can always rely on the Bergman to stay cool.

His sub-zero breath turned any part of the pitch it touched into **smooth, glossy sheets of ice**. In an instant, there was a long pathway of *slippery ice* beneath the monster ball. I shivered as the temperature dropped well below what was safe weather in which to be wearing shorts.

But at least the monster ball was having fun. **'WHOOOOOOOPS! HAHAHAHAHAHA! WHEEEEEE!'** it cried with delight as it slipped and slid down the icy path on its bottom. (Do monster balls have bottoms?)

Then the **FANGTOMS'** star player, Vulfgang Werewolf, finally pounced.

He leapt on to the ice path and began *sliding* effortlessly along in pursuit of the monster ball. He was **grinning broadly and looking as relaxed as if he were out for a leisurely afternoon at the ice rink.**

Even I was impressed as he extended one hairy leg behind him like a ballet dancer, spread his clawed arms wide and **whipped** into a *reverse-triple-spin-jump.* He pirouetted through the air, his mane flowing out behind him as though he were in a *shampoo* commercial. He landed right beside the monster ball and, with a *cheeky flourish of his claws,* sent a spray of ice into the monster ball's face and stopped its slide.

50% of the crowd **roared** in admiration of his skating abilities and hair, while at least another 30% **roared** their admiration of his hair alone. (Which, to be fair, was perfect.)

Even the monster ball applauded.

After pausing to run one *manicured paw through his extravagantly coiffured hair,* Vulfgang booted the monster ball straight towards the wide open goal. The **BAT-PACK** arced me up and alongside it. It looked as if nothing could stop the **FANGTOMS** from scoring and winning the **MONSTERBALL** Cup Final.

But the **ALL-STARS'** Stenchman and Buzz-Bomber had other plans.

They swung into what was clearly a well-practised move. The tiny bat-winged bat-wielding monster emitted an *ear-bleeding screech* and dived towards the ground like a starving hawk that has just spotted a well-fed hamster in a back garden.

Down below, the Stenchman heard the screech. I watched in disbelief as he **seized hold of the hair on the top of his own head and yanked firmly upwards.** There was a horrible **SCHKLOOOP** noise as the Stenchman *plucked his own head from his shoulders.*

Then he tossed it up into the path of the diving Buzz-Bomber. She swooped in at full speed, swung her bat and connected with the Stenchman's head. It shot across the pitch, straight towards the goal-bound monster ball and *cannoned* into it from the left.

The monster ball **ricocheted** off course, missing the goal completely. Instead, it shot straight towards me. **I barely had time to scream** before dodging safely out of the way, and the ball flew right off the edge of the pitch. It banged into the glass spectator screen and dropped to the floor, out of play, **giggling happily to itself.** Meanwhile, the Stenchman's head spun up and disappeared over the top of the crowd barrier.

The crowd cheered and groaned in unison.

I dropped to the touchline to help the doctor guide the Stenchman (or what remained of him) off the pitch.

'Can he still play?' I shouted over the crowd's deafening cheers and boos.

'If you can get this crowd to give you his head back,' yelled the doctor, **'I can stitch it on again.'**

'Oh, there's no chance of that,' croaked the passing Bergman. As he spoke his cold blast of breath floated off across the pitch like a small cloud of damp fog. 'I saw him play that trick three seasons ago – a fan caught his head and refused to give it back. In the end the **ALL-STARS'** manager had to buy it back off **eeeeBay.'**

BODY PARTS – VARIOUS

HEAD [STENCHMAN]

Some signs of wear. Reasonable offers over K3000 considered

Buy it now for **K3400**

POSTAGE FREE to all dimensions (except 419)

FANGTOMS 0
ALL-STARS 0
(Retired injured: the Stenchman)

I restarted the match.

This time Vulfgang Werewolf kicked off for the **FANGTOMS.** Unfortunately, he ran straight through one of the Bergman's cold, damp breath clouds, and **his enormous hair instantly collapsed**. It flopped down across both his eyes, making the werewolf **miss-kick** the monster ball, which skittered off at a right angle and bounced across one of the **piranha ponds.** The fish inside took one look at the size of the passing monster ball's teeth and decided to leave it well alone, so it landed back on the pitch and **bobbled** into the open space between the two teams.

Everyone raced after it. I hovered over the **ALL-STARS'** Toeknee Stomper as he *bounded* ahead on his tiptoes, while the **FANGTOMS'** Rock-o-Dile **scurried** straight towards him from the opposite direction as fast **as his little legs could carry him.**

I briefly wondered why the **FANGTOMS'** fastest player, Vulfgang Werewolf, wasn't chasing. But, glancing back across the pitch, I could see he was far too busy *repairing his deflated coiffure.* Cameras zoomed all around him as he used his *pocket hair dryer, comb and styling product to quickly rebuild his trademark hair style.* (All the time ensuring maximum product placement for his **BIG-HAIRY** brand of hair products.)

It was clear that Rock-o-Dile was no match for
Toeknee Stomper. The **ALL-STARS** player was
just that little bit **lighter** on his toes
(which wasn't surprising
as he was all
toes).

So in a last act of desperation Rock-o-Dile flung
himself at the ball, his jaws gaping wide open and
then snapping shut.

SNNNAAAAPPPPP!

'AAAARRRRRGGGGGGGGHHHHHH!'

Unfortunately Rock-o-Dile had bitten down too
late – Toeknee had already kicked the monster
ball out of the way and Rock-o's teeth were now
clamped like a vice round Toeknee's trademarked
STOMPSTARᵀ designer boot, which held his
celebrated big toe.

I blew my *whiztle* to stop the play and dropped down to the pitch to aid the injured players. The doctor came bounding across the blue grass.

'LET GO! LET GO! LET GO OF MY TOE!' screamed Toeknee.

'I can't!' mumbled Rock-o-Dile irritatedly through his closed mouth. **'It's pure muscle instinct!** It'll take at least half an hour for the muscles to relax.'

'Don't worry,' said the doctor as she pulled an improbably large No.25 syringe from somewhere about her person. 'I'll give them both a sedative. **It'll help Toeknee with the pain and relax Rock-o's jaws.'**

A few minutes later, both players had been carried back to the team dugouts and were snoring peacefully. I helped the doctor get ready to *prise open Rock-o's jaws by fetching a car jack and a heavy-duty crowbar from Lance.*

'Will they be all right?' I asked.

'Toeknee will need a few days off his foot,' said the doctor as she *inserted one end of the crowbar into Rock-o's tightly locked jaws.* 'But I'm afraid they're both out for the rest of this match. There's nothing more you can do here. You may as well get on with the game **before the crowd starts to riot.'**

FANGTOMS 0
ALL-STARS 0
(Retired injured: the Stenchman, Toeknee Stomper, Rock-o-Dile)

'THERE'S A HOLE IN MY TUMMY'

Chapter 11

The rule book said that to keep things fair after a **simultaneous injury,** the match must be restarted with a dropped-ball.

'Is it OK to pick you up?' I asked the monster ball.

As a general rule I find it is always a **good idea** to ask a monster's permission before touching them. For one thing, it is polite. For another, **it's very sensible when the monster has just eaten someone else half an hour ago.**

'Of course it is, Ref!' The monster ball laughed as my **BAT-PACK** carried us both up to about a hundred and fifty feet above the pitch. 'I must say I am very impressed with your performance so far. **I'm enjoying myself enormously!'**

I blew my *whiztle* and dropped the monster ball to the waiting monsters below. **Unfortunately,** it landed on the one player who wasn't paying attention at the time: Vulfgang Werewolf.

He was far too busy **Insta-Twitt-Booking** pictures of his freshly repaired hairstyle to his **thirty-three million followers on anti-social media.** So it came as a complete shock when a monster ball landed right on his now perfect coiffure. By the time I'd got back down to pitch height, he was in a right state.

'**AAAAAARGHHH!'** he yelped. '**GET IT OFF ME! GET IT OFF ME!'**

The monster ball tutted loudly at this over-reaction.

'**Oh, calm down, you big puppy!**' it said. 'I don't even like the taste of hair . . .' But then it paused and sniffed. *'Wait . . . what's that delicious smell?'*

It licked Vulfgang's hair experimentally. Then it smiled broadly and smacked its enormous lips.

'**Ooooooh!**' it said. '**I DO like the taste of your hair product, though.**' And with that the ball began to suck up the vain werewolf's luscious locks as if they were hairy spaghetti.

'**HELP! HELP! HELP!**' yelled Vulfgang.

He waved his paws frantically at the monster ball, which didn't do anything apart from **send dozens of pictures of his hair being eaten** to his thirty-three million followers on anti-social media.

Those pictures were instantly **trending.**

'Hold on! We'll help you!' cried his teammate, Venus the flytrap. I got well out of the way as the snapping heads of Vita, Violet and Veggie all darted in. Each one grabbed on to the parts of Wolfgang's hair that the monster ball hadn't yet consumed. 'Let go of Wulfie at once!' they demanded, pulling together as hard as they could.

'GAGGGHHGHHH! I CAN'T,' gagged the monster ball. It was coughing like a cat with a furball. 'His horrible fluffy fur is stuck in my throat.'

But the Venuses weren't quitting. If anything, they yanked harder. Vulfgang's hair was now caught in a **tug-of-war** between Venus and the monster ball.

I briefly considered intervening. But I doubted any of this was against the rules, and if I did say something there was a distinct possibility of me **losing one or more of my limbs.** So I decided to wait and see how it played out.

'OW! OW! OW! HOWWWWW-OOOOOOOOOOO!' howled Vulfgang. **'BE CAREFUL!** Or you'll pull it o—'

RRRRIIIIIIIIIP' There came a sound like *Velcro ripping apart* and Vulfgang Werewolf's *trademarked hair came away from his head* in one piece. Beneath it was a completely normal and scruffy werewolf mane. The forty thousand **MØNSTERBALL** fans in the stadium instantly went silent.

'I KNEW IT!' cried the doctor from the touchline. 'No one could possibly have hair that perfect.' She tutted. 'To give teenage werewolves such *unrealistic expectations of physical beauty . . .'* But before anyone could take in this *bouffant bombshell,* the hideously embarrassed Vulfgang had bounded across the pitch and bolted into the team dressing rooms.

I marked him down in my notebook as:
'Retired voluntarily'.

But Vulfgang's famous hair was still in the game.

The monster ball was now regretting its decision to try to eat it. **The hair was now firmly stuck in its throat,** and could be neither **swallowed** nor **spat out.** The Venus triplets had seized their chance and had begun to slowly drag the resisting monster ball across the pitch and towards the goal.

'GAGGHH! GET OFF ME!' growled the struggling monster ball. But it was too late. The Venus triplets were soon joined in the tug-of-hair by their teammate, the Bat-in-the-Hat. He grasped Violet, Vita and Veggie round their collective waist and flapped his powerful cloak to pull away.

'C'MON! WE'VE GOT IT NOW!' he cackled, and together they were slightly stronger than the resisting monster ball. It was like one of those **life-or-death struggles** that takes place on the dusty plains of the Serengeti, or round Grandma

Zimmer's house on a Sunday afternoon when she battles my dog, Piglet, for possession of her false leg.

Every single eye, eye-stalk, ear and other bizarre sensory apparatus was utterly focused on the action.

So no one noticed the Buzz-Bomber's sneak attack from above.

She had intended to use surprise, her maximum speed and a **VERY** big bat to whack the monster ball clear across the pitch and into the goal, thereby winning the match for the **ALL-STARS** in a single stroke.

And it would have worked too.

That is if, at that very last second, the **tug-o-hair** struggle hadn't suddenly swung in the monster ball's favour. The Bat-in-the-Hat was jerked forward, straight into the path of the Buzz-Bomber's swing. **The shocked vampire took the full force of the blow.**

THWAAACK!

The Bat-in-the-Hat pinged backwards across the pitch as if he were on the end of a **bungee** cord, and **smashed** straight into the **ALL-STARS'** rather slow-moving wooden defender, Twiggy.

There was a loud CRRRASSSSHHH that was reminiscent of the time my dad stuck his foot through the roof of our brand-new shed. (Although with a lot less bad language.) *Shards and splinters of wood went everywhere.*

Two of them left very **worrying** holes in my shorts, while one gave me an **unpleasant centre-parting.**

Twiggy, alas, wasn't so lucky. She stood there, swaying, with a large **vampire-shaped hole** in her trunk.

I blew my *whiztle* to stop the match immediately.

'Are you all right, Twiggy?' I asked.

'There's a vampire-shaped hole in my tummy,' boomed the hollow voice of the giant plant, as if I somehow might not have noticed. 'I think I'll have a bit of a lie-down.' She promptly felled over. But I wasn't worried for her – it was just shock. Tree-monsters are excellent at **re-growing** missing bits. And when they can't, there are some excellent **cosmetic carpenters** around.

The doctor was once again on the pitch, tending to the injured Bat-in-the-Hat.

The **FANGTOM** winger looked like a **VAMPIRE PIN-CUSHION.** There were dozens and dozens of tiny wooden splinters protruding from him.

'AAAARGHHH!' he cried in terror. **'STAKES! STAKES! STAKES!'** The doctor plucked one of the splinters out – it was the size of a cocktail stick.

'Don't panic,' she said reassuringly. 'They're mostly tiny and none of them are anywhere near your heart. If you can sit nice and still, **I'll get cracking with my tweezers.'**

```
FANGTOMS   0
ALL-STARS  0
(Retired injured: The Stenchman,
Toeknee Stomper, Rock-o-Dile,
the Bat-in-the-Hat, Twiggy.)
(Retired voluntarily: Vulfgang
Werewolf.)
```

NOT A POPULAR MOVE

Chapter 12

Back on the pitch the Buzz-Bomber and Venus were **arguing furiously.**

The Buzz-Bomber spotted me and appealed loudly. 'Ref! Please tell this **perambulating pineapple** that what I did was legal.'

I pulled the thick little **M⊕NSTERBALL** rule book out and rifled quickly through the pages. It took a while to find the relevant section marked, 'BATS: Their specification, use and misuse.'

And I was still puzzling on why Rule 21A said that *human hockey sticks were banned as 'far too dangerous'* when I found Rule 21D.

There was no doubt about it. The Buzz-Bomber's blow was legal. **I broke the bad news to Venus.**

'But look what this **witless weapon-waving waspish wazzock** has done to our teammate,' snapped Vita, gesturing at the Bat-in-the-Hat.

'How **DARE** you call me a **WASP?**' the Buzz-Bomber asked in outrage. **'I'll have you know that my mother was a fruit fly and my father was a flying monkey.** There's no waspishness in our family!

Take that back!'

I rushed between them. 'Now, now!' I said calmly. 'I am sure Buzz-Bomber didn't mean for this to happen. It was all an acci—'

'Of course she did!' sneered the Violet head. It was starting to **twitch angrily.** 'And will you please get that INSECT to stop BUZZING around me and stand still for a second? *I am finding it EXTREMELY hard to CONTROL my instinctive desire to just SNAP HER UP!*'

'Snap me up, will you?' said the increasingly irritated Buzz-Bomber loudly. 'You think you're fast enough to snap me up?' And, rather unwisely, she began BUZZING noisily round and round Venus's three heads, taunting her with, **'Can't catch me! Can't catch me! Can't cat—'**

The Violet head flashed out and **snapped** up the Buzz-Bomber.

'LET ME OUT OF HERE! You VICIOUS VEGETABLE!' yelled the Buzz-Bomber.

Her hands rattled Violet's teeth as if they were prison bars.

'Shan't!' said Violet sulkily. 'I warned you not to buzz me.'

Vita and Veggie rallied to her support. 'I'm sorry, Ref,' said Veggie. 'But we can't be held responsible for our actions around fast-moving insects.' Vita nodded.

I consulted my rule book once more.

'I'm sorry,' I said to Venus, digging the **infra-RED card** from my short's pocket. 'I'm afraid I'm going to have to send you all off.'

RULE 44:
Players must not eat any other players or any part of any other player. The breaking of Rule 44 is punishable by instant sending off the pitch.

An instant later it was **complete pandemonium.**
The **FANGTOMS** players and manager were all
protesting Venus being sent off. The **ALL-STARS**
players and manager were protesting the Buzz-
Bomber being **falsely imprisoned. Everyone was
shouting at once.** And, to make matters worse,
behind the security screen forty thousand monsters
were **booing, cheering, stomping, screeching,
whinnying, honking, gurgling, braying,
farting and roaring.** There was even some
annoying twerp playing a **vuvuzela.**

I couldn't hear myself think over the deafening chants of:

'FANGTOMS FOREVER! FANGTOMS FOREVER!'

And 'AWFUL ALL-STARS! AWFUL ALL-STARS!'

Suddenly it was all too much for me. What on earth was I trying to do? A human couldn't referee a **MONSTERBALL** match! I'd had enough.

'FANGTOMS FOREVER!'

'AWFUL ALL-STARS!'

I was just about to take off my **BAT-PACK**, hand back the *whiztle* and walk back to Lance when I felt the monster doctor's hand on my shoulder.

'AT TIMES LIKE THIS,' she bellowed into my ear, 'I FIND IT VERY HELPFUL TO ASK MYSELF, "WHAT WOULD MY MOTHER DO?"'

That seemed like an odd suggestion as I was fairly sure my mother had never refereed an *anarchic event* with out of control irrational monsters shouting and bellowing loudly at each other.

But then I realized I was mistaken.

She'd been refereeing my family for years.

I took a deep breath and tried to remember what *special techniques* my mum had developed over the years for dealing with moments of **complete chaos and mayhem** in our house. Moments like when the rest of the family are **singing tunelessly along with Piglet** at the top of our voices as he howls at all the dogs in TV commercials.

And suddenly the answer popped into my head.

I switched on my referee's lapel mic. There was a loud **CLICK!** and a brief hum of feedback that said I was now connected to the **100,000KW PA system** of the **MONSTERBALL** Cup Final.

I tried to emulate Mum's most menacing tone of voice. *'QUIIIIIIIIIEEEEEEEET!'* I yelled as loudly as I could.

The stadium quaked.

Forty thousand shocked (and slightly scared) monsters instantly fell silent. Even the annoying vuvuzela player stopped. **'RIGHT!'** I said, my voice **BOOMING** and **REVERBERATING** around the stadium. 'LISTEN TO ME! MONSTERBALL is YOUR game. NOT MINE! And according to YOUR rules, Venus has to be sent off for **unauthorized eating.** And since she won't let the Buzz-Bomber go she's out of the game too. I will be restarting the match in two minutes. THAT IS ALL.'

Then I switched the mic off.

The crowd was silent, apart from a few thousand mumbling voices. Even Krakatoer and the Bergman, the only two players left in the game, looked slightly in awe of me as they *shuffled obediently* to take their places on the pitch.

CRAZED REF TERRIFIES FANS

I said a mental thank you to my mum.

'Well done, Ozzy!' said the doctor. 'I see that **monster-assertiveness** training course I sent you on has paid off. **Your monster handling skills are coming along very nicely.** We'll soon have you standing up to Delores!'

I doubted that. Standing up to forty thousand baying monsters was one thing. Arguing with Delores was in a different league entirely.

FANGTOMS 0
ALL-STARS 0
(Retired injured: The Stenchman, Toeknee Stomper, Rock-o-Dile, the Bat-in-the-Hat, Twiggy.)
(Retired voluntarily: Vulfgang Werewolf.)
(Sent off: Venus the Snapper.)

'I MEAN, LITERALLY!'

Chapter 13

Two minutes later Krakatoer and the Bergman were waiting at opposite ends of the pitch.

I was *hovering* over the centre circle of the field, looking down at the monster ball beaming excitedly up at me.

'Are you ready?' I asked.

'Oh, **ABSOLUTELY!**' the monster ball said. 'I'm having a blast. **I haven't had this much fun since the Cup Final of 1217 BCE,** when the match organizers decided to **electrify** the whole pitch.'

Well, at least the monster ball was enjoying itself amidst all this chaos. I was just hoping that **nothing else dangerous could happen** now that there were only two players left on the pitch.

FANGTOMS!
FANGTOMS!
FANGTOMS!
FANGTOMS!
FANGTOMS!
FANGTOMS!
FANGTOMS!
FANGTOMS!
FANGTOMS!

At my *whiztle* the Bergman charged in from the **FANGTOM** end, skating forward on a path of his own icy breath. *He quickly gathered speed,* until he was as **unstoppable** as a **ski-jumping hippo.**

Krakatoer erupted from the **ALL-STAR** end. She scorched across the grass, powered by an **effective stream of molten lava shooting out of her rear end.**

ALL-STARS!

ALL-STARS!

ALL-STARS!

ALL-STARS!

ALL-STARS!

ALL-STARS!

ALL-STARS!

Whoever got to the ball first would win.

It was a game of chicken – surely one of them would back off at the last second? I didn't know what would happen if lava crashed into ice, but a *vague memory* from my physics class told me that it probably wasn't good to be nearby when it happened.

But the crowd didn't care. They just **roared** encouragement to their players.

'FANGTOMS FOREVER!'

'AWFUL ALL-STARS!'

Krakatoer and the Bergman *accelerated* towards each other, *moving faster and faster and faster every second.*

'FANGTOMS FOREVER!'

'AWFUL ALL-STARS!'

At this point it became terrifyingly obvious that neither player was going to stop.

'FANGTOMS FOREVER!'

'AWFUL ALL-STARS!'

The sensible part of my brain decided that it had been ignored for long enough. It seized the controls to my body and insisted **(very, very firmly)** that we move away to a safer distance.

I sent urgent signals to the **BAT-PACK** to get me as

far away from the impact site as possible.
I was still *ZOOMING* back across the pitch,
towards the safety of the dugouts,
**when the Krakatoer
and the Bergman
collided into each
other.**

There was a **blinding flash** of light,
a **shockwave** and an **enormous** impact.
The entire **MONSTERBALL** stadium **bounced**
around for a bit, as if someone were fiddling around
with the control knob for this dimension's gravity.

Then, when the shaking finally stopped, I realized that the air had become as **thick, hot and sweaty** as the *Swamp Spa treatment room*.

The doctor appeared through the steam, mopping her forehead with a length of **mummy bandage.**

'Where did all this steam come from?' I asked her.

'Oh, this is the Bergman,' she said, staring up with a look of amazement as the steam began to rise up and out of the stadium.

'The heat from the impact with Krakatoer has transformed his icy body straight into a gas – without passing through the intervening liquid stage. It's actually quite *sublime* if you think about it.'

It sounded quite concerning to me. 'Will he be all right?' I asked.

'He'll be fine,' said the doctor confidently. 'Look, he's already **pulling himself together.'**

She was right.

We watched as the steam began to form a small cumulonimbus-shaped cloud. The wind caught it and blew it slowly away over the top of the safety screen.

'He'll be right as rain later this evening,' observed the doctor, 'then back at team HQ the day after. **Unlike poor Krakatoer.'** She led me over to the centre of the pitch where, at the base of a huge newly created crater, was a **large grey stone obelisk.**

'Is that Krakatoer?' I asked.

'Yes,' the doctor replied sadly. She produced a **small geologist's hammer** from one of her **infinite pockets** and started tapping the statue on its head and listening carefully. 'I'd say approximately **97% granite, 2.9% silica and 0.1% pumice,'** she mused. 'Melting all that ice extinguished her flame and cooled her to a more primitive **non-lava** form. Perfectly safe of course, but she won't be able to move again until she is re-melted in the family volcano. Failing that, we can always drop her in the **atomic reactor at the University of East Ugglia's canteen.'**

But something was wrong.

There was something very important missing. Something that I felt sure was essential in order to play a game of **M⦿NSTERBALL...**

'Monster ball!' I cried. 'Where's the monster ball? Did the explosion destroy it?'

The doctor laughed. **'You can't destroy a monster ball!'** she said. 'It's totally impossible – **like trying to scrape dried-on breakfast cereal off a bowl.'**

'Then where has it gone?' I asked.

The doctor clearly had no idea.

She turned and bellowed, **'HAVE ANY OF YOU LOT SEEN THE MONSTER BALL?'** at the dugouts. The remaining players and managers were just emerging from wherever they had dived for cover from the **explosion.** Veggie, Vita and Violet peered out from the nearby No.5 corner hole, but it was the Buzz-Bomber who **screeched** excitedly from her toothy prison.

'THERE!' she yelled. One tiny claw pointed out excitedly from between Violet's jagged teeth.

She was pointing straight upwards.

'Where?' said the doctor and I in unison. We gazed up at a bright green sky that was empty of everything except pale purple clouds, and a tiny, tiny, tiny black dot.

'Is that a bird?' I asked.

'I don't know,' mused the doctor. 'Maybe a plane?'

'No! You idiots,' snapped the Buzz-Bomber (who had excellent sight despite having only one eye). 'It's the monster ball!'

I squinted harder at the dot – it WAS the monster ball.

'The explosion must have blasted it straight up into the stratosphere,' said the doctor excitedly. 'And now it's falling back to Earth!'

Even the crowd had noticed it by now. And behind the security screen all the chattering and screeching had stopped as forty thousand monsters gazed up at the falling monster ball in silence.

And as it hurtled towards the ground I noticed that the ball had its tiny little arms stuck out to either side. For some reason it was flapping them, but was having about as much success as a sky-diving ostrich. And as it dropped below five hundred feet the monster ball's mad cackling laugh sang out across the silence of the stadium.

'**HAHAHAHAHAHAHAHAHAHAHAHA!**' it
cried. '**I'M FLYING! I'M FLYING! I'M FLYING!**'

It wasn't really flying of course. It was more
like dropping in a very specific direction. And by
pure chance (or skill) that direction happened to
be straight towards the *wide open mouth of the
waiting net below.*

At two hundred and fifty feet the ball began to yell, **'GOOOOAAAA...'** At one hundred feet it added **'...AAAL-LLLLLLLLL!'**

And at zero feet, forty thousand stunned and silent monster spectators watched as the monster ball flew straight into the open stringy mouth of the goal. It lay there in the net laughing and shouting, **'GOOOAAAAAAAALLLLLLLLL! Ha ha! I actually scored a goal! With myself! HAHAHA!'** Its squeaky voice rang out across the silent pitch. Then the surviving players rushed to surround me.

'Does the goal count?' asked the Bat-in-the-Hat. He was now free of all but the smallest splinters.

'And, if so, then which team **ACTUALLY** scored it?' demanded Veggie.

'Izz the match over?' slurred a still woozy referee from a bench. 'Who won?' she added, before passing out again.

'Obviously the team whose player touched the monster ball last,' said the Buzz-Bomber irritably from her prison inside Violet's mouth.

'Which means it was me,' said Vita. 'I touched it when I was pulling on Wulfie's hair.'

Vulfgang Werewolf had slunk back into the dugout wearing a **large floppy hat and dark sunglasses.**

'I think you'll find, **ACTUALLY,** that I vas the last player to kick the ball. Therefore the FANGTOMS wi—'

'Complete compost!' boomed Twiggy. She paused from nailing temporary planks of wood over the hole in her tummy. 'The last touch was obviously the Stenchman's head. His brilliant *ricochet* shot means the **ALL-STARS** win!'

The zombie troll's headless body lurched up off the bench in triumphant agreement, but promptly ran straight through the wall of the dugouts.

'Actually,' said the doctor, dropping the last of the Bat-in-the-Hat's splinters into a waste bin, 'the last individual to touch the ball was the referee when he placed it on the centre spot. Perhaps he scored?' She winked at me.

The players and managers of both teams were all suddenly united in **horror** at the idea that a human could score in a **MØNSTERBALL** match. They began **snorting, howling, barking, hissing** and **buzzing** so loudly that I had to shout to make them hear me.

'NO! NO! NO!'

I insisted. 'Rule 3 is **VERY** specific about that.'

RULE 3:
A goal is scored when a monster 'encourages' the monster ball into the net.

'A goal can only be scored by a monster.

And sadly –' I pretended to be deeply disappointed about this – 'I'm not a monster.'

'So which team won, then, Ref?' asked the still sleepy Toeknee Stomper. 'There were only two monsters on the pitch. It must have been one of them.'

'Well . . . not necessarily,' I mused. 'I think you might have forgotten that there was another monster on the pitch at the time.'

The players looked blankly at me for a moment. But then, when they followed my gaze to where the **grinning monster ball** swung lazily in the goal's netting, the penny finally dropped.

Vulfgang blurted, 'But you cannot POSSIBLУ mean that the monster ball won the match?'

'Of course I mean the monster ball,' I said. **'Are you denying that the monster ball is a monster?'**

They couldn't.

'So are you suggesting that the monster ball didn't score the goal?' I asked.

They weren't. They'd all seen it sort of 'fly' into the goal with their own eyes. So before any of them could object I seized my chance. I flipped on my lapel mic, connected to the stadium's huge PA system and made an announcement in as loud and confident a voice as I could manage.

After an EXTENSIVE consultation of the rule book I have decided that the goal is valid. Which means that the official winner of the 297th MONSTERBALL Cup Final (Dimension 3) is . . .

the monster ball!

You could have heard a splinter drop.

Forty thousand monsters simultaneously said, **'HUH?'** and began to mutter angrily amongst themselves.

'Which means,' I quickly added, 'that the **FANGTOMS** didn't lose to the **ALL-STARS.** And the **ALL-STARS** didn't lose to the **FANGTOMS.'**

With this **face-saving manoeuvre,** the stadium was filled with a ripple of *polite applause.*

And with the monster ball safe inside the net, even the *Old Gods*™ seemed to finally accept the result.

In a nursing home somewhere in Dimension 5.3 a button was pressed. **'GOAAAAAALLLLLLLLL!'** announced the automated electronic scoreboard. **More horns blew than in a clown-car traffic jam.** So many **fireworks erupted** from the stands behind the security screen that they would have constituted a **small regional war** back on Dimension 3.142.

And with the official result announced, hundreds of tiny camera parasites suddenly swarmed over the spectator security screen. Flashbulbs exploded in the players' faces and the travelling swarm of **monster locust journalists** descended with pages of pointless questions for everyone.

CARNIVEROUS CARS ONLY

HONK!

HONK!

Pundits parachuted in and began to prattle on and on and on about nothing. Microphones were thrust into the faces of all the players and managers (and where they didn't have faces, whichever hole they spoke out of).

In the **complete pandemonium** that followed, the doctor took me by the elbow and quietly guided me away towards Lance.

'Well played, Ozzy,' she said as we climbed unnoticed back into the comfortably familiar cab of our monster ambulance. 'I think you have earned a lovely hot cup of bile tea and a **triple chocolate brawnie.**'

That sounded wonderful. '**But can I PLEASE take these ridiculous shorts off now?**'

'Of course,' she said. 'Though I don't know why – you have excellent legs.'

I AGREE . . .

said Bruce.

THEY REMIND ME OF A GIANT SPIDER SUPERMODEL I ONCE DATED.

'When you're quite finished, Bruce,' said the doctor, 'please take us back to the surgery. But take us a long route back.'

'Why?' I asked.

'Well, it'll take a while to **unpick you out of those shorts,**' she said. 'But more importantly we'll need the journey back to put our heads together and work out **how we're going to explain the result to Delores and Vlad.**'

THE END

Extract from an article in *WHAK-O!*
the bestselling monster sports
daily newspaper:

WHAK-O

MONSTER BAL
MONSTERBAl

BALL USES BALL TO SCORE GOAL! RESULT TO STAND, DESPITE PROTESTS FROM THE PHILOSOPHY DEPT AT THE UNIVERSITY OF EAST UGGLIA.

The most extraordinary game of MONSTERBALL took place yesterday. Not since the notorious final that was disrupted by a plague of zombie triffids has there been as much controversy in a single match. The incredible events began when the referee was eaten by the monster ball. Chaos ensued until the monster doctor and his human assistant arrived when...

STORY CONTINUES INSIDE!

THE BEST-SELLING SPORT IN 5 DIMENSIONS
WINS CUP
DETAILS ON PAGES 1,2,3,4,5,6,7,8,9,10-35

GLOSSARY

Bat-pack: The reason prehistoric vampires lived in deep dark caves was not — as many believe — because they were afraid of the sun. They were actually terrified of being carried off in the claws of the giant and vicious Gargantu-Bat.

Emerging after thousands of years of cowardly skulking in caves, vampires discovered their hated predator had gone extinct due to lack of prey.

The Gargantu-Bat's only remaining descendent, the BAT-PACK, has none of its ancestor's homicidal personality but still retains the jolly useful 'picking-up-monsters-and-carrying-them-away' instinct.

Big Spring-in-a-Box (BSB): Famous monster inventor Greta Hideer built the very first BSB in order to play a practical joke on her husband. When the emergency services finally recovered him from a nearby skyscraper's roof, Greta realized that her invention had enormous commercial potential.

The BSB was an instant bestseller. And is still popular for teaching baby monsters to fly and getting rid of door-to-door salesmen.

Commercials: Short films made to convince monsters that one bottle of stink water is better than any other.

Coughee: A hot beverage made by boiling the roasted poo pellets of the Spleurrrrrgh snake. Although enjoyed by some monsters, coughee is not as popular as bile tea, mainly because it's made by boiling the roasted poo pellets of the Spleurrrrrgh snake.

Eenie-meenie-micro-second: A period of time so incredibly short that it is difficult for instruments to measure. It is approximately the time it takes between a toddler dropping their ice-cream and beginning to wail.

Frumious bandersnatch: An infamous monster who claimed that shouting rude and unfunny things at other monsters was hilariously funny. The bandersnatch was exiled to Dimension 2.6 where it now presents a late-night comedy news show.

Hairy dimension (Dimension 4.8): Dimension 4.8 is home to a strange and hairless race of gods known as the Oldbaldians, who are completely obsessed with hairdressing. They insist that all visitors passing through Dimension 4.8 must consent to being temporarily 'styled' by the Oldbaldians.

Fortunately all hair styling reverts to normal upon exit.

Lava-juggling: Lava-juggling is EXTREMELY dangerous. It should never be attempted without fully fire-proof P.P.E. underwear rated up to 3,000 degrees Celsius, and a comprehensive home fire insurance policy. Monsters with an interest in juggling are advised to begin with safer objects like hungry piranhas or Grotweiller puppies.

Lawless dimension: Dimension 2.6's combination of lawlessness and flaming hot lava beaches make it very popular with thrill-seeking tourists and ex-politicians on the run.

Leg-warmers: Reptilian monsters often suffer from very cold legs. Cosy woollen leg-warmers can solve this problem, but they should only be worn indoors, otherwise the wearer runs the risk of arrest by the notoriously strict inter-dimensional fashion police.

Monster Twister: This is far more complicated than the human version of Twister, as monster bodies often have dozens of limbs and / or tentacles. This means games of Monster Twister often end up looking like the horrible tangle of cables behind your TV unit in the living room.

Zombies are forbidden from playing Monster Twister for the obvious reason that they can cheat.

Monster locust journalists: Enormous swarms of these creatures descend on areas unlucky enough to have something 'interesting' happen. Without an immediate response from the locals (anti-journalist spray or a strong hosepipe are both effective), infestations can last for weeks and severely damage property prices.

Primitive: There is a huge amount of debate about which is the most primitive form of monster. Some suggest the monamoeba. (See *Monster Doctor: Slime Crime*.) Others note the two-inch long snot-gobbler that lives entirely on discarded bogies. Occasionally these debates get very lively — or break out into small wars — but at least all monsters can console themselves that they are more advanced than human beings.

Stompstar: Toeknee Stomper's brand of sports footwear. Not only are they cheaper than Wolfgang Werewolf's luxury *BIG HAIRY* brand, but STOMPSTAR shoes have the advantage of being sold not only in singles, but also in multipacks of twelve for monsters with multiple limbs.

Sky-diving ostriches: Ostriches are surprisingly keen on sky-diving. Bird-brain psychologists think it might have something to do with jealousy of their more showy flying cousins.

Sadly, ostriches often botch their landing by instinctively coming in head-first.

The school stampede scandal: The professional do-gooders at C.R.U.S.H. (Campaign to Reduce Unnecessary School Hospitalizations) work tirelessly to prevent deadly school stampede incidents by installing wider school doorways on days when popular desserts are served.

To help avoid further tragedies, please give generously at Wwmw.stopsquishingkids.com.

Trending: A complex mathematical algorithm. It allows a social media user to know which topic is currently best avoided.

Whiztle: A tube-shaped little monster that is so ticklish it emits an ear-splitting screech of joy if blown into. This sound is audible across almost every known frequency and impossible to ignore. It is therefore perfect for sporting events and as a birthday present for the children of people who really annoy you.

Ziggy: Ziggy Toescratcher was a former assistant of Dr Annie Von Sichertall. His cheerful personality and ability to deal with Delores made him very popular. The fact that his fur was very soft and calming to stroke helped too.

Ziggy is currently studying to be a monster doctor at the University of East Ugglia. When qualified, he hopes to take up a residency in the large bowel department.

Read on for a sneak peak at Ozzy and the
monster doctor's first adventure,

The Monster Doctor!

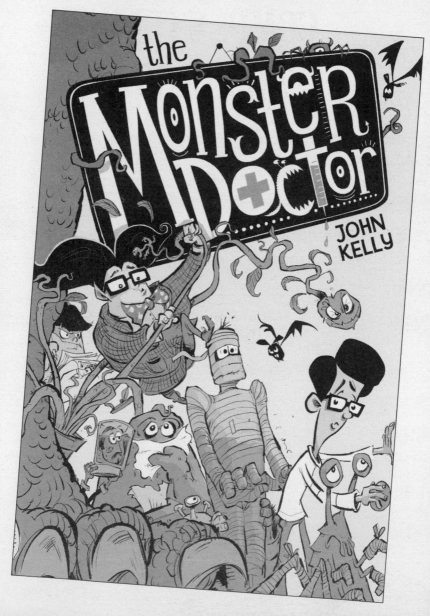

COMPLETELY 'ARMLESS

Chapter 1

I was walking down the street one morning when the man in front of me **dropped his left arm** on the pavement.

Now, I don't know about you – maybe where you live people are **always** dropping limbs on the ground in front of you.

shuffle

shuffle

1

Who knows, maybe you can't walk to the shops without tripping over a **leg** or an **ear** or a **chin,** but, I can assure you, that's not the kind of thing you see every day around here. Oh no! Around here people drop normal things, like pens, bus passes or ice creams.

Not an **arm.**

But there it was, on the pavement at my feet.

A complete left arm.

The man who'd dropped it was just walking away. He was pretty scruffy, but that's no excuse to go dropping arms all over the place, is it? For one thing, the council will probably fine you for **littering.**

(Do body parts count as litter? I don't know. But I wouldn't google that if I were you.)

Anyway, I'm quite a helpful person (and not very **squeamish**) so I picked up the arm and went after him. I resisted the temptation to wave at him with it – that would have been **rude.** Luckily, the man hadn't got too far. In fact, he was shuffling so slowly down the pavement that catching up to him was really easy.

I tapped him on the shoulder. 'Excuse me,' I said, 'but I think you've dropped something!'

He stopped dead in his tracks and turned to face me. I was right about him being scruffy. He looked as if he hadn't had a bath in a year or two and **several of his teeth were missing.**

Then I noticed that his teeth (and his arm) weren't the only things missing.

Somehow he had managed to lose one of his **ears** as well.

And an **eye.**

And quite a big chunk of his **nose.**

'Hello, young man,' he said with a smile. 'Can I help you?' He seemed very friendly – though he was well overdue for a trip to the dentist.

I held out the left arm he'd dropped. 'I think this belongs to you,' I said.

He looked confused for a moment as he counted all the arms in front of him. There were **three** (which was one more than there really should have been). The penny dropped and he noticed his own arm was missing.

'Silly me!' he said.

ACKNOWLEDGEMENTS

I'd like to thank the following people
for this latest collection of silliness.

My wife Cathy, whose extraordinary ability
to devour an entire bag of tortillas in one
go was the inspiration for the monsterball.

My agents Jodie, Emily and Molly at
United Agents, for putting up with my
whinging for so long.

And Cate, Rachel, Sue and Amanda
at Macmillan for making these books look
so good (and contain so few spellin
miztakes and tiepows).

ABOUT THE AUTHOR

John Kelly is the author and
illustrator of picture books such as
The Beastly Pirates and *Fixer*, the
author of picture books *Can I Join
Your Club* and *Hibernation Hotel*, and
the illustrator of fiction series such
as Ivy Pocket and Araminta Spook.
He has twice been shortlisted for the
Kate Greenaway prize, with *Scoop!*
and *Guess Who's Coming for Dinner*.
The Monster Doctor is his first author-
illustrator middle-grade fiction series.